For Marnie
M. K.

First American edition published in 2008 by Boxer Books Limited.

Distributed in the United States and Canada by Sterling Publishing Co., Inc.
387 Park Avenue South, New York, NY 10016-8810
First published in Great Britain in 2008 by Boxer Books Limited.

www.boxerbooks.com

ISBN-13: 978-1-906250-09-6

1 3 5 7 9 10 8 6 4 2

Printed in China

All of our papers are sourced from
managed forests and renewable resources.

THE Big Bell and THE Little Bell

Music and Lyrics
Martin Kalmanoff

Illustrated by
Alastair Graham

Boxer Books

Welcome to the tiny kingdom of Calvinopolis. The sleepy moon rests in a canopy of stars, illuminating this tranquil land on an oh-so-cold and frosty night. But then . . .

BONGGGG!

The big bell breaks the peace of gentle
night-time with its huge and angry sound.
Even the sleepy moon is awakened with a start.

"Why is the big bell so loud, Mama?" asks Kitten.

"Because it thinks it is very important!" says Mama.

And Kitten sings:

"'Those who make the biggest noise aren't always
as important as they think!'

"Tell me the story again, please, Mama?" asks Kitten.

"The story of the big bell and the little bell?

Of course, Kitten," says Mama.

Kitten snuggles up and Mama whispers,

"Are you ready, Kitten?"

"Yes, Mama," Kitten whispers back.

"Good," says Mama, "then I'll begin . . ."

A big bell sounds
like a mighty gong,

And a little bell just makes a tiny clink.

But those who make the biggest noise
Aren't always as important as they think.
Oh, long ago in a distant land . . .

On the day they were
crowning the king,
The great big bell went

"BONG,
BONG,
BONG!"

And the little bell
just went "bing."

The big bell said to the little bell,
"I don't see why you bother to ring,
'Cause I make a great big

BONG,
BONG,
BONG!

But all you can do
is go bing."

The king said,
"Stop the big bell,
And heed what I have to say.

Go and tell the little bell
I command it to play
on my wedding day."

So remember that making
a great big noise
Is not the important thing.
'Cause the king got a headache
from the BONG,
BONG,
BONG!

But he loved the little bell
that just went **"bing."**

Yes, a great big bell
makes a mighty sound,

And a little bell just makes a tiny clink.

But as you can see . . .

Those who make the biggest noise

Aren't always as important as

they think.

Mama gently closed the book.

Kitten slept peacefully in the moonlit room.

All was quiet.

"Bing!" went the little bell in the distance.

"Good night," said Mama. "Sweet dreams."